Dinosaur Are the Best!

Adapted by Ximena Hastings
Based on the screenplay "Moms' Campout" written by Elise Allen
Based on the television series created by Craig Bartlett

Simon Spotlight
New York   London   Toronto   Sydney   New Delhi

SIMON SPOTLIGHT
An imprint of Simon & Schuster Children's Publishing Division
1230 Avenue of the Americas, New York, New York 10020
This Simon Spotlight paperback edition March 2019
© 2019 The Jim Henson Company. JIM HENSON'S mark & logo, DINOSAUR TRAIN mark & logo,
characters, and elements are trademarks of The Jim Henson Company. All Rights Reserved.
All rights reserved, including the right of reproduction in whole or in part in any form.
SIMON SPOTLIGHT and colophon are registered trademarks of Simon & Schuster, Inc.
For information about special discounts for bulk purchases, please contact Simon & Schuster Special
Sales at 1-866-506-1949 or business@simonandschuster.com.
Manufactured in the United States of America 0219 LAK
10 9 8 7 6 5 4 3 2 1
ISBN 978-1-5344-3082-2 (pbk)
ISBN 978-1-5344-3083-9 (eBook)

It was a very special day for the Pteranodon family. While Mom cleaned the nest, the kids played pretend camping trip and collected nature treasures, like leaves and shells.

Since the kids were having such a great time, Mom decided they should go on a real camping trip!

Dad was away on a fishing trip, so it would just be the kids and Mom.
   Suddenly, Don had an even better idea: Why not invite all the
dinosaur kids and their moms?
   It would be a special moms' campout!
   They all cheered and agreed to spread the word. They would meet at
the Dinosaur Train and head off to the Big Pond!

Everyone boarded the Dinosaur Train. Annie was already thinking about a wild camping adventure. Mikey and Tiny were excited too— being tiny would not stop them from having a fun adventure.

"All aboard!" called Mr. Conductor.

"Wait," cried Buddy. "Tank and his mom were supposed to come too!"

At that moment, Tank and his mom, Trudy, arrived with plenty of food for the trip.

Now everyone was ready to go on their campout!

The Dinosaur Train took off toward the Big Pond as Mr. Conductor collected tickets and heard about their moms' campout.

"I remember when I was a wee little Troodon, I'd go camping with my mother," he said. "She had the best ideas for camping games."

He told them that one of the games they used to play was called the Nature Connection Game.

"Mother always said you can't appreciate nature just by looking at it," said Mr. Conductor. "You need to climb around, dig in, splash about, get dirty, and look at things in a whole new way! Then you make a real nature connection."

"How does the Nature Connection Game work?" Mom asked.

"Well, it's really whatever you want it to be, as long as it gets you involved with nature," said Mr. Conductor.

He explained that one of the ways to make a nature connection is to think like an animal. You choose an animal and act like it to better understand it.

"If you pretend to be an animal, you probably understand why it has all its features," said Buddy.

"Excellent hypothesis, Buddy," said Mr. Conductor.

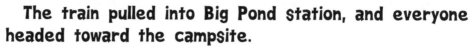

The train pulled into Big Pond station, and everyone headed toward the campsite.

After setting up, Mom asked the group, "What does everyone think? Should we play the Nature Connection Game first?"

"Yes!" exclaimed Don.

Since Mr. Conductor said their game could be whatever they wanted, Don invented one called The Hole Truth.

The game was simple: First you had to dig a hole, and then you had to find buried treasures. Everyone started digging!

Annie and her mom, Dolores, dug big holes and found seashells. Tank and Trudy found delicious roots!

Mikey and his mom found squirmy bugs and fuzzy plants in a log. Don found the perfect place to rest. The kids and their moms were making real nature connections!

The group gathered around to play the next game. This time they wanted to play the one Mr. Conductor had suggested: Think Like an Animal.

The moms decided to watch as the kids found animals to imitate.

Annie pretended to be a frog. "Ribbit, Ribbit," she said as she jumped around.

"You make a really good frog, Annie," said Don.

"But the real frog jumps so far," observed Tiny. "How does she do that?"

"I know! It's her long legs and light body!" said Annie. "I never knew it was such hard work being a frog!"

Tank pretended to be a worm.
Tank observed that worms could crawl and eat grass at the same time, just like a Triceratops!

Mikey pretended to be a turtle—except his shell was a log.
His mom loved the extra protection and safety his log shell offered.

Buddy and Mom went flying over the Big Pond.

"Buzz, buzz, buzz," said Buddy. He was pretending to be a bee.

Mom's wings made a whooshing sound as she flew.

"I bet bees also make noise with their wings, and that's why they buzz!" said Buddy.

Everyone had learned something new about each animal by observing their different features!

The moms joined the kids for the next game, which was called Barking Up the Right Tree.

This game involved closing your eyes, feeling a feature from a tree, and saying what you felt.

Everyone closed their eyes. Shiny called out, "Ready? Bark!"

Dolores and Annie felt that the tree was "rough"!
"Smooth!" called out Mikey and his mom as they flew around another tree's trunk. Mom and Tiny rubbed their backs against a tree and said it felt "bumpy."

Don asked them to identify how the branches of the trees felt.

"Leafy!" called Dolores.

"Slippery," said Annie.

"Long and huge!" cried Mikey and his mom as they glided past branches.

Buddy asked them to say what the leaves felt like.

"The leaves feel pointy," observed Tiny.

"Thick!" called out Mom.

Tank and his mom said every feature of their tree was simply delicious!

"Every tree is different, even if they look the same," said Buddy.

The last Nature Connection Game of the day was called Making a Splash.

All the kids got together with their moms to throw rocks in the Big Pond.

Together, Trudy and Annie carried a large rock to make a big splash.

Mikey and his mom flew up high and threw a small rock. The small rock fell from so high that it made an even bigger splash than the big rock!

Tank and Trudy weren't afraid to get dirty—they found a muddy rock and pushed it into the Big Pond.

Mom and Shiny had a different idea, and they surprised everyone by flying high, high, high up above the Big Pond and diving in at full speed!

Everyone had a great day playing nature connection games with their moms.

"We should do more moms' camping trips. This was the best day ever," said Tiny.

"I'm glad you all had fun," said Mom. "We did too."

"Mr. Conductor would be proud that we made real nature connections," said Buddy.

"And some other great connections too," said Mom.

After a great day at the Big Pond, the kids settled in for bed under the stars and wished their moms a good night. Moms are the best!

Get to know the dinosaur moms from this book!

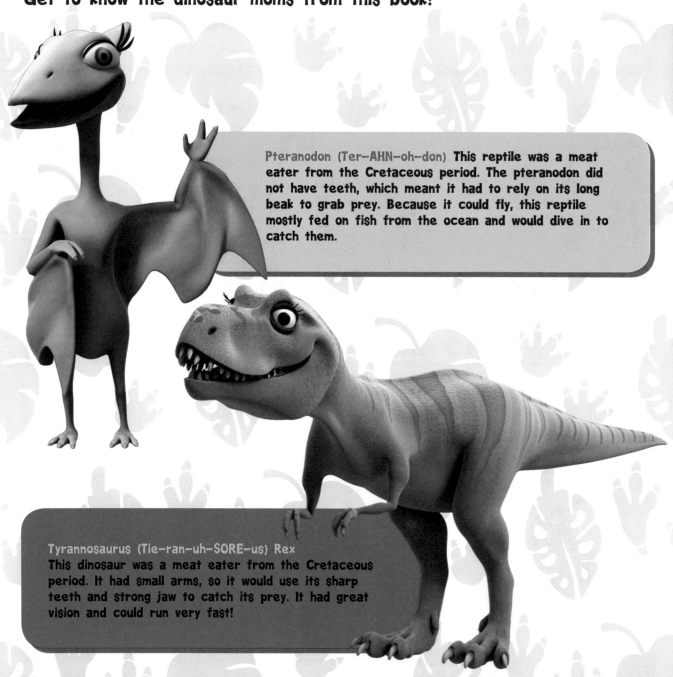

Pteranodon (Ter–AHN–oh–don) This reptile was a meat eater from the Cretaceous period. The pteranodon did not have teeth, which meant it had to rely on its long beak to grab prey. Because it could fly, this reptile mostly fed on fish from the ocean and would dive in to catch them.

Tyrannosaurus (Tie–ran–uh–SORE–us) Rex
This dinosaur was a meat eater from the Cretaceous period. It had small arms, so it would use its sharp teeth and strong jaw to catch its prey. It had great vision and could run very fast!

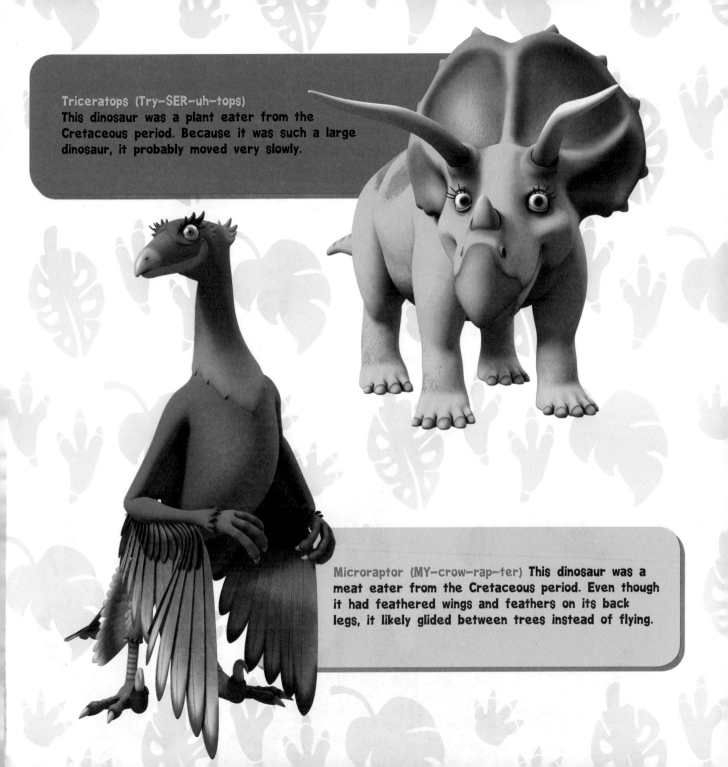

Triceratops (Try-SER-uh-tops)
This dinosaur was a plant eater from the Cretaceous period. Because it was such a large dinosaur, it probably moved very slowly.

Microraptor (MY-crow-rap-ter) This dinosaur was a meat eater from the Cretaceous period. Even though it had feathered wings and feathers on its back legs, it likely glided between trees instead of flying.

It's fun to go outside and make nature connections. When you play outside, what kinds of things do you like to do? What do the trees look like? How does the grass feel? Do you see any insects crawling on the ground or flying in the air? Next time you go outside, talk to your parents, caregivers, or friends about what you see around you, and ask them about what they see. Isn't nature exciting?